PUFFIN BOOKS

DEAR DUMB DIARY,

Let's pretend this NEVER happened

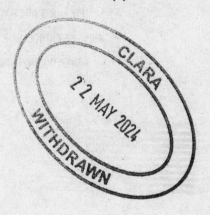

More of Jamie Kelly's diaries

LET'S PRETEND THIS NEVER HAPPENED

MY PANTS ARE HAUNTED!

AM I THE PRINCESS OR THE FROG?

NEVER DO ANYTHING, EVER

DEAR DUMB DIARY,

Let's pretend this NEVER happened

Jim Benton

The (nearly) true confessions of Jamie Kelly

PUFFIN

PUFFIN BOOKS

Published by the Penguin Group
Penguin Books Ltd, 80 Strand, London WC2R ORL, England
Penguin Group (USA) Inc., 375 Hudson Street, New York, New York 10014, USA
Penguin Group (Canada), 90 Eglinton Avenue East, Suite 700, Toronto, Ontario, Canada M4P 2Y3
(a division of Pearson Penguin Canada Inc.)
Penguin Ireland, 25 St Stephen's Green, Dublin 2, Ireland (a division of Penguin Books Ltd)
Penguin Group (Australia), 250 Camberwell Road, Camberwell, Victoria 3124, Australia
(a division of Pearson Australia Group Pty Ltd)
Penguin Books India Pvt Ltd, 11 Community Centre, Panchsheel Park, New Delhi – 110 017, India
Penguin Group (NZ), 67 Apollo Drive, Rosedale, Auckland 0632, New Zealand
(a division of Pearson New Zealand Ltd)
Penguin Books (South Africa) (Pty) Ltd, 24 Sturdee Avenue, Rosebank,
Johannesburg 2196, South Africa

Penguin Books Ltd, Registered Offices: 80 Strand, London WC2R ORL, England

puffinbooks.com

First published in the USA by Scholastic Inc. 2004
Published in Great Britain in Puffin Books 2011

005

Text and illustrations copyright © Jim Benton, 2004
The moral right of the author/illustrator has been asserted
All rights reserved

Set in 16/18pt Tarzana
Printed in Great Britain by Clays Ltd, St Ives plc

British Library Cataloguing in Publication Data
A CIP catalogue record for this book is available from the British Library

ISBN: 978-0-141-33578-0

www.greenpenguin.co.uk

MIX
Paper from
responsible sources
FSC   FSC™ C018179
www.fsc.org

Penguin Books is committed to a sustainable
future for our business, our readers and our planet.
This book is made from Forest Stewardship
Council™ certified paper.

For
everybody that is in,
or will be in,
or has ever been in,
middle school.

Special thanks to: Craig Walker, Steve Scott, Susan Jeffers Casel, Shannon Penney.

And especially to editor Maria Barbo who really and truly knows her way around middle school.

This DIARY PROPERTY OF

Jamie Kelly

SCHOOL: MACKEREL MIDDLE SCHOOL

LOCKER: 101

BEST FRIEND: Isabella

PET: Stinker which is a beagle

EYE COLOUR: Green

HAIR COLOUR: ~~Brown~~ Brownishly Blonde with Brunette Brownness

WARNING

READ NO FURTHER

The
Last
Person
Who
Kept
Reading →

THIS IS NOT
YOUR DIARY

I CAN TELL

Dear Whoever Is Reading My Dumb Diary,

Are you sure you're supposed to be reading somebody else's diary? Maybe I told you that you could, so that's okay. But if you are Angeline, I did NOT give you permission, so stop it.

If you are my parents, then YES, I know that I am not allowed to call people idiots and fools and goons and halfwits and pinheads and all that, but this is a diary, and I didn't actually "call" them anything. I *wrote* it. And if you punish me for it then I will know that you read my diary, which I am *not* giving you permission to do.

Now, by the power vested in me, I do promise that everything in this diary is true or, at least, as true as I think it needs to be.

Signed,

Jamie Kelly

PS: If this is you, Angeline, reading this, then HA-HA! I got you! For I have written this in poison ink on a special poison paper, and you had better run and call 911 right now!

PPS: If this is you, Hudson, reading this, I have an antidote to the poison and it is conveniently available to you through a simple phone call to my house. But don't mention the poison thing to my parents if they answer. I think they might be all weird about me poisoning people.

Here they ARE
DISAPPROVING POISONING

Monday 02

Dear Dumb Diary,

I was out playing with my beagle, Stinker, this afternoon and I was doing that thing where you pretend to throw the ball and then don't throw it and Stinker starts running for it until he realizes you didn't really throw it at all. Usually I only do it two or three times, but today I guess I was thinking about something else because, when I finally realized that I hadn't thrown the ball yet, I had probably done it about a hundred and forty times. Stinker was a little bit cross-eyed and foamy and he wouldn't come back into the house for a long time.

I wonder if dogs can hold a grudge.

Frustration
Foam

Tuesday 03

Dear Dumb Diary,

I think I was very nearly *nicknamed* today, which is almost the worst thing that can happen to you in middle school. I was eating a peach at lunch and another peach fell out of my bag onto the floor, and Mike Pinsetti, who only breathes through his mouth, was standing there and he said, "Hey, Peach Girl."

He's pretty much the official nicknamer of the school, and Pinsetti's labels, although stupid, often stick. (Don't believe me, Diary? Just ask old "Butt Buttlington", who was one of Pinsetti's very first nicknames. I don't even know his real name. Nobody does. He's been called Butt Buttlington for so long that his mom actually called him Butt by accident one time when she dropped him off at school. "Bye, Butt Buttlington," she said. Then, when she realized what she had done, she tried to make it better by following up with: "We're proud of you.")

One second Before
You Get A Nickname

One Second After
You Get A Nickname

Back to my peach story. I picked the backstabbing fruit up real quick. I thought nobody had heard Pinsetti, which pretty much cancels out a nickname. But then this adorable musical laughter that sounds like somebody is tickling a baby by rubbing its tummy with a puppy comes from behind me. When I turn round, I see it's none other than Angeline, who was probably evilly committing this nickname to memory.

It's only a matter of time before I have to start signing my homework as **PEACH GIRL**.

3

Wednesday 04

Dear Dumb Diary,

   Today Hudson Rivers (eighth cutest guy in my grade) talked to me in the hall. Normally, this would have no effect on me at all, since there is still a chance that Cute Guys One Through Seven might actually talk to me one day. But, when Hudson said, "Hey," today, I could tell that he was totally in love with me, and I felt that I had an obligation to be irresistible for his benefit.

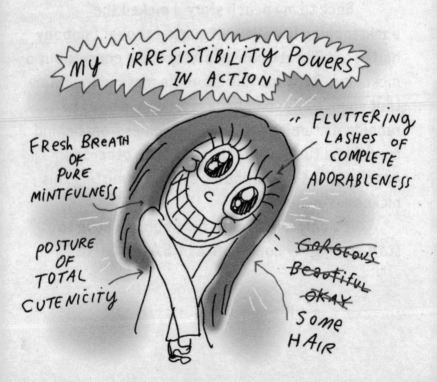

MY IRRESISTIBILITY POWERS IN ACTION

FRESH BREATH OF PURE MINTFULNESS

FLUTTERING LASHES OF COMPLETE ADORABLENESS

POSTURE OF TOTAL CUTENICITY

~~GORGEOUS~~ ~~Beautiful~~ ~~OKAY~~ SOME HAIR

So, just as I'm about to say something cool back to Hudson (maybe even something **REALLY** cool — we'll never know for sure now), Angeline comes round the corner with her jillion cute things dangling from her backpack, and intentionally looks cute **RIGHT IN FRONT OF HIS EYES.** This scorpion-like behaviour on her part made me forget what I was going to say, so the only thing that came out of my mouth was a gush of air without any words in it. Not like this mattered, because he was staring at Angeline the same way Stinker was staring at the ball a couple of days ago.

STINKER   HUDSON

It was pretty obvious that all of his love for me was squirting out of his ears all over the floor. Ask Isabella if you don't believe me. She was standing right there.

As if that wasn't vicious enough, get this:

He says to Angeline: "Wow, is that your Lip Smacker I smell? ChocoMint? It's great."

Angeline stops for just a second and **LOOKS RIGHT AT ISABELLA AND ME.** Then she says to Hudson, "Yeah, it is." And her radiant smile freezes him in his tracks.

Frankly, I think that it is just rude and obscene to have teeth white enough to hurt and maybe **PERMANENTLY DAMAGE** the eyes of onlookers.

AAAAAAGH!!

Sizzle

HAZARDOUS DAZZLING WHITENESS RAYS

(In case my children are reading this years from now, this is the exact moment Angeline stole your father, Hudson, from me, and it is her fault that now your last name is Rumpelstiltskin or Schwarzenegger or Buttlington.)

SAD SAD FUTURE BABY LEARNING that his fatheR has been STOLEN

DUMB DIARY

Angeline's fault

Here's the thing: Isabella is the *ONLY* girl in the entire school who uses ChocoMint Lip Smacker. It's the grossest flavour they ever made, but she *needed* her very own unique Lip Smacker flavour, and so she settled on the only one nobody else likes. All the girls know it's hers. Even Angeline knows it.

So, Dumb Diary, let's see that scene again in slow motion: suddenly, in one swift move, Angeline had stolen my future prom date/boyfriend/ husband, and Isabella had lost her signature Lip Smacker scent. (Isabella would rather wear her grandma's giant-bottomed pants to school than let anyone think she is copying Angeline.)

A MYSTERY of NATURE

ISABELLA'S HUMAN- SIZED BUTT

ISABELLA'S GRANDMA'S HORSE-LIKE BUTT

I suppose I could have said something, but I knew that Angeline had the "Peach Girl" nickname loaded in her Imaginary Slingshot of Pure Wickedness and was ready to let me have it right in front of Hudson.

I was powerless.

Of course, Dumb Diary, you understand that I'm DESTROYED. What you may not fully appreciate is the impact this scandalous event is having on Isabella. She is EXTREMELY smell-oriented, and not really well equipped to change her scented ointments. I foresee a long, painful bout with chapped lips in her future.

It also occurs to me, Dumb Diary, that Angeline is so perfect that the word "perfect" is probably not perfect enough for her. One day they'll have to invent another word for her and when they do I hope it rhymes with vomit or turd because I think I have a good idea for a song if they do.

PRINCESS
TURD
OF
TURDSYLVANia

Wednesday 04, The Evening Edition

Dear Dumb Diary,

Tonight at dinner, Mom announced that we're going to be taking care of my little cousin in a few weeks. He's, like, my aunt's daughter's brother's nephew or something.

I know that your uncle's kids are your cousins, but then there are things like first cousins and second cousins and cousins once-removed. What does that mean? "Cousins once-removed."

I had a wart once removed.

cousin
once-removed

wart
once removed

And, Dumb Diary, just to update you on Mom's Latest Food Crime, last night she made a casserole with 147 ingredients, and it still tasted bad. It's hard to believe that out of 147 ingredients not one of them tasted good.

Of course I ate it anyway. If you don't eat it, Mom gives you the speech on hard work and how the hungry children in Wheretheheckistan would just love her casserole.

It seems to me the kids in Wheretheheckistan have enough problems without dumping Mom's casseroles on them, too.

Thursday 05

Dear Dumb Diary,

Because of Angeline, who thinks she is the Prettiest Girl in the World but probably is not even in the top five, I had to buy my lunch at school today. I just could not take the chance that my mom would pack a peach in my lunch again and then, while I was secretly trying to throw it in the trash, Pinsetti or Angeline would spot it and cause a big Nickname Event. Then I'd have to run away from home.

And just to prove that the entire Universe is on the side of evil, perfect Angeline, it was Meat Loaf Day in the cafeteria. Thursday is always Meat Loaf Day. The cafeteria monitor, Miss Bruntford, takes it personally when you don't eat something. And she gives us all kinds of grief, in particular when we don't eat the greasy cafeteria meat loaf.

Note supernatural resemblance of Bruntford to meatloaf

Miss Bruntford starts going, "What's wrong with the meat loaf?" and her giant slab of neck flubber starts waggling all over the place. She has one of those big, jiggly necks that looks like it might be soft and fluffy like the meringue on top of a lemon meringue pie.

So I had no choice but to eat some of the meat loaf, which smells a little like a wet cat, and that is Angeline's fault, too, as is everything.

Poke

One time a kid touched her NECK-FLUB AND DOCTORS DECLARED Him MEDICALLY GROSSED OUT.

Friday 06

Dear Dumb Diary,

I don't know if I've ever mentioned Angeline before, but she's this girl at my school who is beautiful and popular and has hair the colour of spun gold as if anybody likes that colour.

Isabella and I were in the hallway today, and Isabella insanely tried to engage Angeline in conversation as she walked by, which was way out of line for Isabella since Angeline is like a "9" in popularity while Isabella is hovering around an unsteady "5". (And after Isabella's lip-balm-dependent lips start decaying from Lip Smacker withdrawal, who knows how low that number could go?)

Anyway, Angeline just kind of looks at Isabella as if she's something peculiar and mildly gross like an inside-out nostril, and, without saying a word, Angeline just keeps walking.

ISABELLA

Have you **EVER** known somebody like Angeline, Diary? Like, maybe at the store where I bought you there was some other really expensive diary that thought it was so cool that it walked around the store looking like it had a pen stuck up its binding?

Honestly, Dear Dumb Diary, if there **WAS** a diary like Angeline at the store, and you told me about it, I would go straight to the store and buy it and use its pages to pick up Stinker's you-know-whats when I take him for a walk. But also I would remind you to be happy with who you are, because you are beautiful, and especially to be happy with your own hair, even though you don't have hair. But, you know, that's if you did and if it was real ugly.

ALSO GOOD idea

Goat EATING STUCK-UP DIARY

Isabella later told me that she thought she actually might be able to persuade Angeline to abandon ChocoMint. Isabella is a nice girl and I really like her, but if brains were bananas, let's just say that there would be a lot of skinny monkeys scraping around the inside of Isabella's skull.

Einstein's   Isabella's

DOES YOUR SKULL MONKEY LOOK AS BAD IN A BIKINI AS IT SHOULD?

PS: Nickname Update: nobody has called me Peach Girl . . . *YET*. Angeline must be waiting for just the right time to spring it on me. It is a **KNOWN SCIENTIFIC FACT** that girls who are all pretty and Pure Goodness on the outside are Pure Evil inside.

Angeline is probably just waiting for the exact most embarrassing moment to unveil the Peach Girl nickname to the world.

true person

Saturday 07

Dear Dumb Diary,

Okay, okay. I know what I wrote yesterday about being happy with your own hair colour. Maybe I was trying to be open-minded about accepting people with perfect blonde hair, or maybe I was trying to be a scientist or something, but today I decided to buy one of those hair-dye kits you can use at home. (You probably have never noticed, Dumb Diary, but the truth is: I have some hair issues.)

I picked the one that looked like Angeline's hair colour, which they call "Glorious Heavenly Sunshine". I was not trying to copy Angeline; it just happened to be the first one I grabbed in the fourth store I looked.

I probably should have asked Isabella to help me with the hair dye, but I didn't really want to get a lecture from her about self-acceptance while I pretended not to notice she was afflicted with a rapidly advancing case of what doctors call "Lizard Lips".

I just locked myself in the bathroom and dyed alone.

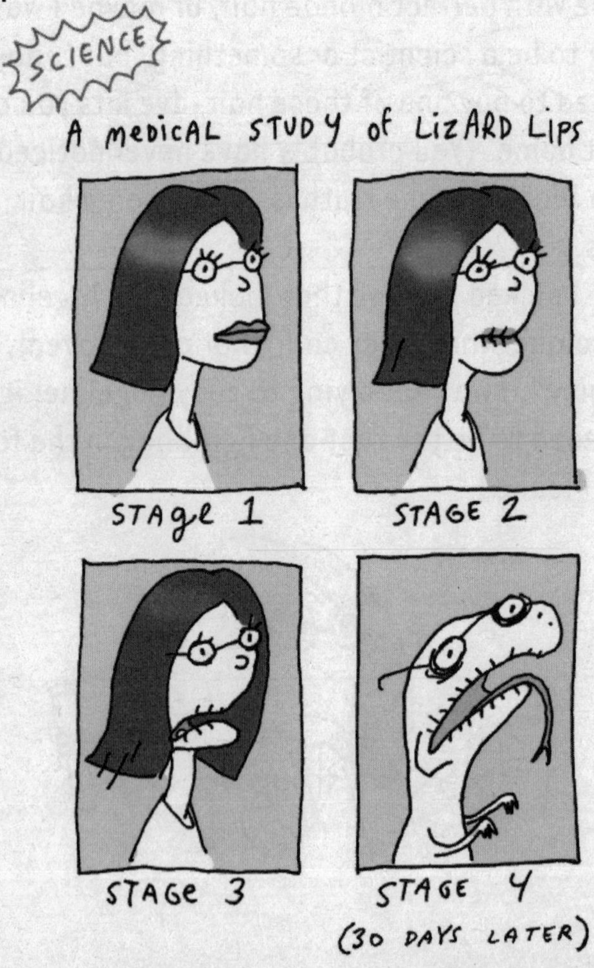

SCIENCE

A MEDICAL STUDY of LIZARD LIPS

STAGE 1

STAGE 2

STAGE 3

STAGE 4
(30 DAYS LATER)

(Which reminds me: I know why they call it "dye". Because after you see what it does, that's what you'll want to do.)

What was supposed to come out as "Glorious Heavenly Sunshine" came out the exact colour of raw chicken. I could have hidden in the poultry case at the supermarket and been perfectly camouflaged.

So now I had to go back to the store and get a kit that would dye my hair back to its original colour before Isabella or my mom could get on my case for not loving myself.

I pulled a clump of my old hair out of my brush so I could match it at the store, which didn't really strike me as gross until I saw how the clerk reacted when I handed it to her to help me find the right colour. Luckily, they had the correct shade, and I brought it home and dyed my hair back.

By the way, you know how the name for Angeline's hair colour is "Glorious Heavenly Sunshine"? The people at the dye company named the one that matches mine "Groundhog".

Sunday 08

Dear Dumb Diary,

Isabella came over much too early today (I was so glad that my hair was back the way that nature had inflicted).

She came over so early, in fact, that she actually saw my dad in his ugly plaid bathrobe that she said looks like he stole it from a homeless zombie, but I think looks *way* worse.

Anyway, Isabella just completed her Loser Scale, which identifies how much of a Loser somebody is, and therefore is a useful guide by which Loser-ness can be measured.

Isabella says that this is how the metric system started: that somebody just like her woke up one day and decided that a litre was a litre and pretty soon everybody agreed (even though nobody knows how much a litre actually is).

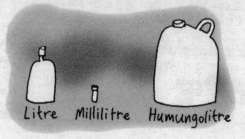

Litre   Millilitre   Humungolitre

Isabella will probably be a Professor of Popularity Science one day.

Here is Isabella's Metric System of Dorkology:

ISABELLA'S
LOSER SCALE
FROM BAD TO WORSE

DINK — PESTY, PARTIALLY STINKY.

DORK — LOUD, OFTEN OAFISH.

DORKBAG — SPITTY-MOUTHED. LIKES TO LIE. TWITCHY.

TURD — MEAN AND THICK-HEADED. QUESTIONABLE SHOE CHOICES.

BLONDEWAD — STEALER OF BALM FLAVOURS. POSSIBLY UNFAMILIAR WITH SOAP.

TURDPIE — BIG-TIME ANNOYING. FUTURE CANNIBAL. UNFLATTERING WARDROBE.

Sunday 08 (late-breaking news)

Dear Dumb Diary,

After Isabella finished making me study her Dorkology System, I talked her into going up to the store to try to choose a new lip-balm flavour. (She SO did not want to do it, but I made her. This sort of Gentle Pressure is part of the grieving process when somebody loses a loved one such as ChocoMint flavouring.)

Even though Isabella made me stand there forever while she rejected about forty perfectly good lip treatments, I had to tell her that the jumbo lip gloss she finally selected and liked was actually a roll-on deodorant.

So the effort was a huge failure, but I'm sorry: friends tell friends they're wearing antiperspirants on their mouths.

EVEN GROSSER THAN it SOUNDS

Monday 09

Dear Dumb Diary,

School was okay today. Actually, it was *better* than okay. Angeline got her long, beautiful hair tangled in one of the jillion things she has dangling from her backpack and the school nurse — who is now one of my main heroes — took a pair of scissors and snipped two feet of silky blonde hair from the left side of her head, so now Angeline only looks like the Prettiest Girl in the World if you're standing on her right. (Although, personally, I think she would look better if I was standing on her neck.)

Also, I got an assignment in English class to do a report on mythology. I asked my teacher Mr Evans what "mythology" meant exactly, and he said it's about things that don't exist. I asked if that would include the hair on the left side of Angeline's head, which got a pretty good laugh from everyone except Mr Evans and Angeline.

Mr Evans said that I pretty much need an A on my mythology report or my grades would be with the mermaids. "You know," he said, "below C level."

Pretty funny, huh? I hope beautiful silky, blond hair grows on his big shiny bald head so that the nurse can cut half of it off.

Tuesday 10

Dear Dumb Diary,

How weird am I?

I had to go down to the school nurse today because I think Mom may have accidentally poisoned me with some sort of mushy noodley stuff we had with dinner last night that tasted almost exactly like socks smell.

I was hoping the nurse could give me some medicine or something, but she couldn't. She just had me lie quietly on a little cot for a while. Evidently, this is how they taught her to unpoison people.

me dying

It was pretty boring, of course, just lying there trying my hardest not to be poisoned, and I started looking around. And that's when I saw it in the wastebasket: a huge clump of long, beautiful blonde hair. **Angeline's** hair.

And here's the weird part: I took it. I don't know why I took it — it's not like I know how to do voodoo against her or anything.

Yet.

I just wanted it.

me escaping with clump

And in case you're worried, Dumb Diary, it turns out I wasn't poisoned after all. The nurse said I probably just had a little "dyspepsia", which I think is the medical way to say that I had a humongous, gigantic amount of gas that could choke a horse.

Wednesday 11

Dear Dumb Diary,

I tried to figure out something to do with Angeline's hair clump today. There's not quite enough to make a decent wig. I thought about planting it like a bush to see if it would grow and grow until I had actually grown another Angeline head. But then I worried it might be more beautiful than the real first head, so forget that.

I guess for now I'll just keep it like a trophy, kind of like you might keep a moose's head on the wall, except that in this case I only got a wad of the moose's hair.

On the subject of her head, Angeline was wearing a little beret on it today to cover up her butchered haircut. (*Beret* is French for stupid hat.) Anyway, nobody could believe how totally goony it looked. I'm sure this will be the end for her and Hudson.

Thursday 12

Dear Dumb Diary,

Like, half the people at school were wearing berets today (including **Hudson**!!!). It's like they were all secret beret-owners, just waiting for a signal from Angeline that it was okay to start wearing their berets. I don't understand it. What if Angeline had accidentally worn her underpants on her head? I think we all know *exactly* what would have happened. Half the school would have been walking around peeking out the leg holes of their boxers.

IDIOT   Buffoon   half-wit

There are only two things about this that really bug me:

1) People only like Angeline because she is totally beautiful and nice and smart.

2) I don't have a beret.

It was Meat Loaf Day again today, like it is every Thursday. The cafeteria monitor, Miss Bruntford, made a big deal (again) about the uneaten meat loaf, but the kids who were wearing their dumb berets were all kind of unified, like the French Resistance, and they just ignored her. This made her even madder, and I noticed that she waggled her neck blubber extra furiously at Angeline, as if she knew that the berets were all Angeline's fault.

WAGGLE WAGGLE WAGGLE

Intense Neck Vibrations actually Register as mild EARTHQUAKE six miles AWAY

SEISMOGRAPH

Food-Crime Update: Mom made something for dinner that was so bad I decided to chance the lecture on Wheretheheckistan and sneak it to Stinker, my beagle. Stinker tried a bite and then, to get the taste out of his mouth, went and ate half of the grit in the cat box.

Now I am a little bit afraid of Stinker, who I think might blame me for how sick he got later, although it was totally Mom's fault, and if he is planning on biting somebody's neck while they sleep it should not be mine. (Dumb Diary, I am saying this out loud as I write so that Stinker can hear me.)

vengeful beagle

Friday 13

Dear Dumb Diary,

It's only about one week until my cousin gets here and Mom and Dad are on **FULL CHILD SAFETY** alert.

They've been putting special indestructible childproof latches on the cabinets where we keep cleaning products and bug killers because, evidentially, little children like to eat them.

Seems like a lot of work. If we don't want kids to eat those things, wouldn't it be simpler to just make them broccoli-flavoured?

Saturday 14

Dear Dumb Diary,

I figured that I had better do something to prepare for the mythology thing in Mr Evans's class.

I went online and read about Medusa, who had poisonous snakes growing out of her head, and who would have been totally jealous of a girl with real hair even if it was the colour of a groundhog.

I have one piece of advice for people with poisonous vipers for hair. Ponytails. Fringe. Something.

BEFORE MAKEOVER

WORN UP IN PROM STYLE

BRAIDS

GLAMOROUS WAVE

I also read about Icarus who made wings out of wax and then flew too close to the sun and they melted. The moral is this: if Icarus had been meant to fly, he would have been born a flight attendant like my cousin Terrence.

Did you know, Dumb Diary, that mythology can include things like trolls and giants and talking fish since it wasn't just the Greeks and Romans that had mythology? Old Dead Guys everywhere had mythology, which I think is very, very interesting to somebody somewhere, maybe.

Finding sunglasses that look cool

is the WORST PART of BEING A CYCLOPS

Saturday 14 (late-breaking news)

Dear Dumb Diary,

Isabella and I were out walking this afternoon and we accidentally walked about a half mile out of our way and *accidentally* found ourselves way over by Derby Street, which was a peculiar coincidence because that is sort of near where Hudson Rivers lives exactly.

Isabella said that walking past his house like this was a form of stalking, but I told her that it wasn't because stalkers are crazy, and we were sane enough to wear disguises.

flawless disguise

The disguises turned out to be a pretty good idea because, as we walked past, Hudson happened to look out the window, which freaked out Isabella who ran — but not before she pushed me down on the lawn.

I caught up to her six blocks later. She apologized, explaining that she only pushed me down before running because of what was probably just an instinct, like if a bear was chasing us.

Since it was only that, I forgave her.

Sunday 15

Dear Dumb Diary,

I finally found a beret at the mall. It cost me thirty bucks, which wiped me out, and I don't even like it, but a fad is a fad and, frankly, I'm not sure if I'm cool enough to ignore a fad. It's a very difficult thing to judge.

I heard about a girl who went to a different school and tried to ignore some huge fad, like cargo pants or something. The next thing you know her family forced her to marry her own first cousin once-removed and she went insane. Although, as I write this, I'm not sure if that has anything to do with cargo pants, and I don't even think the government lets people marry their first cousins whether they are once-removed or not. It's all probably a lie except the cargo pants and insane parts.

me insane

Anyway, I'm tired and it's time for bed. I'm going to try to force myself to dream that a huge toad gobbles up Angeline and then the toad is eaten by a giant hog and then the hog is made into this awful toad-flavoured ham that is served at Angeline's sixteenth birthday party and everybody gets sick including Angeline who is somehow magically alive again to eat her own ghastly toad-hog-ham self.

I don't always remember my dreams, but I'll know if I dream this one because I'll wake up laughing so hard my stomach will hurt.

isn't imagination a lovely thing?

Monday 16

Dear Dumb Diary,

The beret fad is over. As I threw my *thirty-dollar* beret in the trash, I wondered how could it be over so fast. Do you wonder, too, Dumb Diary? Well, stay tuned . . .

Today in science, Mr Tweeds gave us an out-loud pop quiz where he asked everybody one question. This was the question he gave me:

"How could you determine which way north is using only a needle?"

Here is what I answered: "Find a smart person and threaten to stick it in him if he won't tell you which way north is."

Which I guess I knew was wrong, but didn't realize it was wrong enough to get you sent to the principal's office.

And by the way, Diary, here's an easy way to remember if you spell it princi*ple* or princi*pal*. (Maybe you've heard it before, Diary?) Just remember that *pal*eontology is the study of fossils that are about a *jillion* years old.

PALEONTOLOGY   PRINCIPAL

Oh. And by the way: I have solved *The Mystery of the Sudden Demise of the Beret Fad*. On my way to the principal's office I saw that all of the secretary women in the school office were wearing berets.

Thanks a lot, ladies. Maybe next time I'll take a chance on marrying cousin Terrence.

Now get this, **Dumb Diary:** while I was in his office, the principal pulled out the folder containing my permanent record to make a note of this latest smartmouthery. (As you know, your permanent record follows you through school and is not destroyed until you are married or dead or something.) But, when he pulled out my folder, I noticed, just a couple of folders away from mine . . . ANGELINE'S PERMANENT RECORD.

I was MILDLY INTERESTED

Instantly, I knew I had a goal in life: to possess and share the horrible contents of this folder with the world, and to reveal to mankind the boyfriend/scent thief that Angeline really is.

Oops. I got so excited on that last part that I dropped my diary on Stinker's head, who was asleep. And I think he might be swearing in dog language right now.

Tuesday 17

Dear Dumb Diary,

I tried to think about doing something on my mythology report today, since it's getting close to the deadline, and it's probably time to actually make some progress regarding starting to worry about it. I want to work on it, really and truly I do, but I think I may have caught a little case of OCD about Angeline's permanent record.

evil SPiRiT OF ANGELiNE'S FOLDER →

← me innocently trying to do my homework

OCD, in case you've never heard of it, Dumb Diary, stands for Obsessive-Compulsive Disorder, and it's this condition where you become obsessive and compulsive about things. It makes you think about something so much that you do things like wash your hands a hundred times a day, or open your locker over and over to make sure you haven't forgotten anything for your next class, or keep saying over and over to yourself, "I must have Angeline's permanent record."

Anyway, since it's psychological, and not from germs, I'm pretty sure you can catch it from watching a talk show about it, which is how I think I may have caught it. Obviously, Mom will be calling me in sick tomorrow morning.

Oh. And one other thing: Angeline's bald hair patch is almost totally invisible now. She has employed some sort of secret military combing technology to camouflage the patch she had been covering with the beret. It is also possible that she simply regenerated the lost hair, regrowing it the way a lizard regrows a lost tail or a slug regrows — I don't know — a big snotty lump or something that somebody cuts off him.

ANGELINE'S FREAKISH HEAD

BEFORE

AFTER

SINISTER MILITARY SECRET
OR
EVIDENCE OF SUBHUMAN PARENTS?
you decide!

Wednesday 18

Dear Dumb Diary,

Mom would not call me in sick from school today. But it's okay, because I have miraculously recovered from my OCD and actually do not even think about or care about Angeline any more. Let me prove it. Below, I will write the names of people that I just don't care about at all.

George Washington, Ringo Starr, Christina Aguilera, Zeus, Angeline, Dan Rather, Caesar Riley, Angeline, Paul Bunyan, Cleopatra, Nefertiti, Maria Barbo, Angeline, Koko the Signing Gorilla, The Yellow Teletubby, Angeline, Angeline, Angeline, Angeline ANGELINE

Thursday 19

Dear Dumb Diary,

Okay, okay. Maybe Angeline does still bug me a little. I just *had* to have Angeline's permanent record, and the only way to do it was to get sent to the principal's office again.

So at lunch today Miss Bruntford, the neck-waggling cafeteria monitor, lost her mind and said that nobody could leave the cafeteria until they had finished the meat loaf. She was staring at us and we were staring at her and you could have cut the tension with a knife, which is something you can't do with the meat loaf.

SCHOOL IS AN ENDLESS BATTLE
Between the forces of GOOD AND THE
FAT-NECKED FORCES OF EVIL

Suddenly, a big honkin' slab of the shiny slippery meat loaf came flying through the air and smacked Miss Bruntford right in the neck blubber.

She started screaming and sputtering and demanding to know who did it. It seemed like a golden opportunity, so I said that I was the one who had thrown it. Easy ticket to the principal's office, right?

SPLOT

Boxer
SHORTS?
I suspect so.

But get this: as they're hustling me out of the cafeteria like I'm a perp on that *COPS* show, I'm looking down at everybody's trays. I see meat loaf after meat loaf after meat loaf. And then I see one tray without meat loaf. I look up, and there's Angeline, wiping gravy off her hand with a napkin.

ANGELINE!!! She was the one that threw the meat loaf, and I had taken the fall for it.

The GRAVY OF GUILT

Of course, I got a big lecture from the principal and he might have even mentioned Wheretheheckistan. Plus, he banned me from eating school lunches for two weeks. (I got the feeling that he thought that was a much worse punishment than it actually was.)

And, to make things worse, of course I did not get Angeline's permanent record. (I mean, what did I think I was going to do? Knock the principal out with a karate kick and just grab the folder out of the filing cabinet???) It turns out this was a pretty lousy idea. I'm never going to try something that dumb again.

Even if you are justified like I am, kicking a PRINCIPAL'S HEAD OFF is STILL NOT ENTIRELY RIGHT.

Friday 20

Dear Dumb Diary,

I tried something that dumb again. Between classes, I saw the principal talking to Miss Anderson who is a teacher and therefore old, but is beautiful enough to be a waitress, and all the men teachers talk to her for a long time. I ran all the way to the office and walked right in and asked to talk to the principal. He wasn't there, so one of the secretaries told me to come back later, but I told her I had a private matter to discuss with him, and could I leave him a note? Then I told her that with that beret on I thought for a second she was one of the school cheerleaders.

She ACTUALLY Believed it.

Of course, she let me right in and all I had to do was just walk over to the cabinet and snatch Angeline's permanent record. I know what you're thinking, Dumb Diary: you are thinking that I am the Smartest Chick in the World. And you're right. I *am* the Smartest Chick in the World.

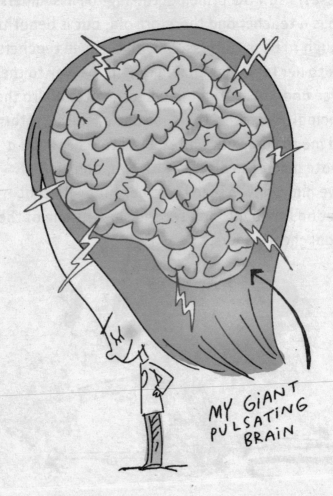

MY GIANT PULSATING BRAIN

And later on, the Smartest Chick in the World forgot Angeline's file at school. On a *Friday*. So now I'll have **OCD** about it all weekend.

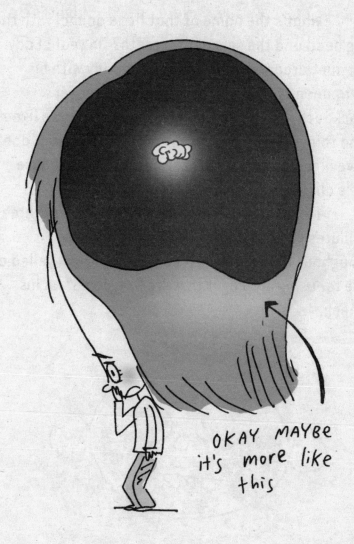

OKAY MAYBE it's more like this

Saturday 21

Dear Dumb Diary,

What's the name of that little animal with the big head and the sharp little teeth? Oh yeah: Eddy. My aunt dropped off Cousin Eddy today with his permanently sticky face and Robot Avenger backpack. She had a big long list of things he liked and things he didn't, but most of all, she said, don't give him anything with strawberries in it because he's allergic.

Mom keeps washing his face, but, like, three minutes later he's sticky again. He's like a doughnut that secretes its own glaze. Mom yelled at me for using my finger to write "wash me" on his cheek.

Sunday 22

Dear Dumb Diary,

Angeline uses such a wonderful and important shampoo that the small wad of hair I have has actually made our whole house smell better. It also has a powerful effect on Eddy, who seems to have an unnatural love for it, and a mutant ability to sniff it out of its hiding places.

My Scientific Theory is that since Eddy will grow up into a Guy one day he is already instinctively and unnaturally in love with Angeline. The hair has no effect on my dad, and Isabella says that is because he is my dad and stopped being a Guy when he met my mom.

The fragrance also seems to have an effect on Stinker, who sneezes and sneezes whenever I grind the hair wad in his face. I wonder if that annoys him?

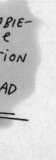

SNARL
GRRR
GRR

ZOMBIE-
LIKE
DEVOTION
TO
HAIR WAD

Monday 23

Dear Dumb Diary,

There's good news and there's bad news. The good news is Mom says that my aunt is picking up Eddy on Thursday, which is a relief because I'm getting tired of trying to hide Angeline's hair wad from him. There's more good news. I remembered to bring Angeline's permanent record home. But I set it down one second and turned my back and when I reached for it again it was gone. I know it was either Stinker or Eddy who took it, but no amount of yelling or depriving of toys or dog bones has had any effect. And Eddy really likes those bones.

WHICH ONE iS GUiLTY?

The mangy flea-Bitten Animal or the dog?

Tuesday 24

Dear Dumb Diary,

It is making me mental that Angeline's permanent record is in this house and I cannot find it. I even looked in Stinker's doghouse, which meant I had to throw out all the sticks and trash he had been keeping in there. Since then, Stinker has been staring at me for hours with his black, black dog eyes and I think he may be planning something against me.

Maybe I should buy a dozen big mean cats to have around the house in case some mean little dog shows up to try to do something mean to me. (Dumb Diary, I read that last sentence out loud so that Stinker could hear it, but it did not seem to have any effect on him. If I turn up missing in the morning, I just hope the police dust for fingerprints, or foot prints, or whatever you call the prints left by those paw-nubs on the bottom of a guilty beagle's foot. Hint, hint.)

BIG MEAN CAT
ARE You GetTing all this, Stinker?

Wednesday 25

Dear Dumb Diary,

    I'm angry on the outside . . .

. . . but I'm far angrier on the inside.

I finally finished my mythology report. In spite of distractions, like Cousin Eddy clawing at the door to get in, and the frustrating knowledge that there could be something so joyfully horrendous in Angeline's folder that it could be used to reduce her to a tiny quivering lump of sobbing goo but I do not know where the folder is.

Happily, Mom told me that Eddy won't be here much longer — my aunt is meeting us at school tomorrow morning to pick him up.

I wonder if I'll miss having him around the house? I didn't miss Stinker's Frantic Itchy Butt Disease when that cleared up, so I think I'll be okay when Eddy is gone.

THE WORLD OF THE BEAGLE
DOES IT REVOLVE ROUND HIS BUTT?

Itches a little

Itches medium

Total freak-out knock-a-table-over itchiness

Asleep but it still itches

Thursday 26

Dear Dumb Diary,

Stinker ate my mythology report.

I guess at least now I know what he's been planning. He was waiting for me to finish it. Here's how I know he was doing it to get back at me: he only ate the words. He left the paper margins in his bowl like pizza crusts.

I had to pack my own lunch this morning, on account of being banned from buying lunch at school. There was only a spoonful of strawberry jam for my sandwich and, just to make things worse, Stinker must have licked it off my bread while I went to the fridge to look for a juice carton. I figured he did it to get the taste of mythology out his mouth — which probably tastes awful — so I didn't even get that mad at him. My mom finished packing my lunch and stuck it in my backpack.

Mythology might taste worse than Mom's cooking

So there I was, Dumb Diary. Mom was dropping me off at school, and I knew I was headed for an 'F' from Mr Evans. I mean, you just can't actually *say* the dog ate your homework. I have to give that mean little beagle credit: Stinker played that one beautifully.

While I was headed into school, my aunt met my mom outside, and they were getting ready to transfer Eddy from one minivan to another when he escaped, I guess.

And the way I know that is because, while I was walking the Walk of the Condemned towards Mr Evans's class, a small, dirty savage went whipping past me in the halls with his little Robot Avenger backpack followed by my screaming aunt. I was just about to grab Eddy for her when I noticed Hudson walking past, and I had to quickly decide if I was going to help a family member or try to look cool for a guy that probably hardly knows I'm alive.

"Hi, Hudson," I said as Eddy scrambled out of sight round the corner, followed by my aunt who I think was starting to cry.

I walked into Mr Evans's class, knowing full well that I would be going first. Mr Evans called on me to stand up in front of the class and give my presentation.

I had just started to say "Mr Evans, I don't have my —" when Eddy ran into the class. His face was swollen and his tongue was so thick I couldn't understand whatever he was jabbering. I suddenly knew that Stinker had not licked my bread this morning — Eddy had. I guess he really *is* allergic to strawberries. Eddy was so puffy he looked like a picture of himself that somebody had drawn on a balloon.

Before   After

Eddy saw my backpack at the same time I saw him use his supernatural hair-wad-locating ability against me, and we both lunged for it. But the little demon-child was faster, and he managed to get his big round head inside the backpack before I could stop him. When I finally pulled his head out, he had Angeline's hair clump stuck like a beard to his always-sticky face. With his dirty clothes and beard and weird swollen-faced jabbering, he didn't seem human.

The fact that I was holding Eddie round his neck as he kicked and growled and clawed at the air did not do much to create the impression that he was a human being, either.

Mr Evans jumped to his feet and turned red and started bulging his forehead vein at us and was all "Do you know this . . . child, Jamie?" That's when I realized that the next thing out of my mouth was going to get me failed, and also nicknamed throughout the school as the Girl with the Crazy Cousin, or something worse: Mike Pinsetti was quickly jotting down a few nickname ideas on a sheet of paper. You could tell he was trying out a few things. I thought about pitching Eddy out the second-storey window.

Then it happened. Eddy had knocked my
lunch bag out of my backpack, and what comes
rolling out and stops right in front of me? A
PEACH. My mom had packed a *peach*.

Angeline stood up. This was it. This was her
big opportunity. She had waited for just the right
moment, and this was obviously **IT**.

Angeline walked to the front of the class, and stood next to me. She smiled her perfect Angeline smile and said, "Mr Evans, Jamie and I did our report together. We did it on trolls. And this," she said, pointing to Eddy, "is our visual aid."

CAN YOU TELL THE COUSIN FROM THE REAL TROLLS?

She didn't call me Peach Girl. She didn't do anything bad. Angeline was **ACTUALLY HELPING ME**. Mr Evans and the whole class — even Hudson — suddenly looked like they were getting this giant backrub from Angeline's voice, which is the most beautiful mortal voice ever heard, but so what?

people melted into puddle of sick love for ANGELINE

My butt was on the line here. So I went with it. The two of us started making it up as we went along and every time Eddy would snarl or growl the whole class would laugh, and I think Eddy even started to like it. I quickly realized this was the best report I had ever given, and I was actually enjoying giving it. Just as we finished, my aunt showed up at the door and took Eddy away, and we got an A on the report and even a round of applause. (Isabella had to do her best not to smile. Her lips are so dry now that even a slight smile will split them open like a pair of burnt hot dogs.)

As I went back to my desk, I asked myself: **Why would Angeline help me out?** Could it have been because I took the fall for her meat loaf crime? Were we supposed to be friends now? The thought of it just made me totally ill. I looked **SO** sick, in fact, that Mr Evans told me to get my stuff and go down to the school nurse.

How COULD EVANS tell that I felt sick?

When I went for my bag, I saw Eddy's Robot Avenger backpack on the floor next to it and, peeking out of just one little corner, I saw Angeline's permanent record. I scooped it up and headed for the nurse's office.

How I tried to Look

How I probably Looked

MY PRECIOUS MY PRECIOUS

The nurse did what she always does. It doesn't matter whether you have a heart attack, a leg eaten off by bear or an axe stuck in your face, it's always the same thing: **Lie Down on the Cot and Rest.**

ILLNESSES OUR NURSE TRIES TO CURE WITH THE COT

HEADACHE

SWALLOWED BY PYTHON

RACCOON MISHAP

NOTHING LEFT BUT SKELETON

While I was lying there, I looked at the cover of Angeline's permanent record. Before I opened it, I amused myself with what might be inside: maybe counterfeiting, kidnapping, fixing the outcome of school football games by means of insincere eyelash-batting at quarterbacks.

Or maybe she had been brought up on charges of spending her whole life as somebody who people can't help but like even though deep down they really and truly want to hate her.

All that was left to do was open it and read it, and then share its terrible contents with the World.

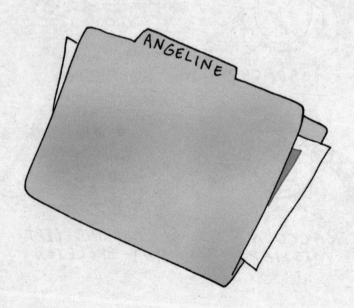

Friday 27

Dear Dumb Diary,

Angeline sat down across from Isabella and me at lunch today. I was eating a ham-and-cheese sandwich that I had packed for lunch but we were all out of cheese, and I had felt guilty about how I had treated Stinker so I had given him the last slice of ham as a truce. I guess you would call it a mustard sandwich if I had remembered to put mustard on it.

Who Doesn't enjoy a nice nothing sandwich?

(By the way, Stinker and I are pals again. I guess he figured that eating my homework had made us even for the last couple of weeks. Thinking back, I suppose that **WAS** fair.)

Okay, back to Angeline (remember Angeline?). Incredibly, between bites of bread, I actually said this to Angeline: "Thanks for saving my life on the report yesterday." I didn't actually intend to be polite. I've been brainwashed by my parents to be polite against my will sometimes.

Then she smiled at me. And it wasn't totally an Aren't-I-Great-with-My-Perfect-Teeth-and-Gums Smile. It was a regular smile. And she said, "We should do something sometime. A movie or something. Maybe you can teach me how to do that thing you do with your hair," she said, pointing at my head. "I can never get my hair to do anything cool."

CONFUSINGLY NON-EVIL

And the very next thing I knew, Dumb Diary, Miss Bruntford the cafeteria monitor had me in a Heimlich position and was trying to disgorge a bread chunk that I had accidentally inhaled when Angeline had complimented my hair. After a couple squeezes, up it came, and I saw Mike Pinsetti standing there, grinning. It was obvious that he had crafted some excellent nickname for me that he was about to unveil, and everybody was waiting to hear what it was going to be when Angeline grabbed him by the collar and said, "Just don't, **PIN-HEADY**."

SQUISH

CHOKING CAN KILL YOU.

HUMILIATION CAN ALMOST MAKE YOU WISH IT HAD.

OINK

SPLAT

PIN-HEADY. It was a masterpiece of nicknaming. It rhymed with his real name, it was insulting and everybody in the cafeteria was standing there to hear it used for the first time. Even though he was utterly shattered, you could see a reluctant respect on Mike's face.

Angeline, who no one even knew had any cruelty within her at all, had shown the meanness that Isabella and I had always known was there.

I sure hope people DON'T WORSHIP me TOO MUCH FOR REVEALING THE TRUTH

Sure, she had only been cruel to Pin-heady (look how I am already forgetting his real name) and, yes, she kind of saved my neck again by not letting him get off a nickname for me, but, c'mon, at least the world now knew that she's not this total perfect angel.

I know what you're thinking, Dumb Diary: use the old one-two punch. I have her permanent record to share with the World. I can fix her once and for all.

Except that I *don't* have it any more.
Yesterday I had decided not to read Angeline's
permanent record. I just slipped out of the nurse's
office and into the principal's office and put it back
in the filing cabinet.

Besides, I thought, this is Angeline, how bad
could it have **REALLY** been?

Isabella's lips cleared up a couple of hours after lunch. It was like a miracle. They turned from what looked like sad little splintered slivers of beef jerky into what look like full, ripe, luscious crescents of papaya.

It was the meat loaf. The mysterious meat it's made from had some sort of incredible healing power on Isabella's lips. And it's her new signature flavour. She stuffed a wad of it into an old lip-balm tube. I know. It's awful. But it smells better than ChocoMint.

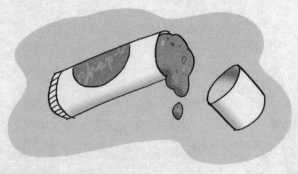

But that was only the second weirdest thing that the Universe did today.

Later on, after school, Angeline walked right up to me.

"I forgot to say thanks," she said.

"For what?" I said.

"For taking the blame for my meat-loafing of the monitor."

And then, when she said that, IT *happened.* I felt the entire Universe groan and creak and shift slightly, and the next thing I knew her terrible Angeline powers were starting to work on me. I felt as though I might be starting to LIKE ANGELINE AGAINST MY WILL.

I told Angeline it was no big deal. I had always wanted to do that myself.

"No, no. It *was* a big deal," she said. "You have no idea how much trouble I would have been in. If you could see what my permanent record looks like, you'd know. One more incident, and I'd be out of here and you'd have Hudson all to yourself, and I am **NOT** going to let that happen." Then she smiled and walked away.

I stood there for a while, Dumb Diary, sort of like a black-eyed beagle who has just seen all of his most precious sticks and trash thrown out by someone who has mistaken him for someone he is not. I was frozen in my spot by feelings of affection and hatred all glopped together like one of Mom's inedible Food Crimes.

Maybe people are like meat loaf: strong medicine, but also deadly poison.

I wondered, as Mike Pinsetti walked by me without making eye contact, if I could find the wisdom that Stinker had found and could exact the precise amount of justice called for here, which was to simply eat Angeline's homework sometime and then call it even.

WELL, IT'S STILL PROBABLY BETTER THAN MOM'S COOKING.

Thanks for listening, Dumb Diary.

Jamie Kelly

**Fancy a sneak peek
at the next Jamie Kelly diary?**

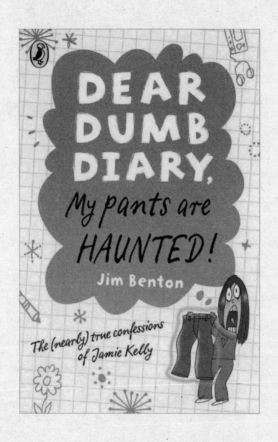

On your own head be it . . .

READ NO FURTHER

UNLESS you are me,

I command you to
Stop reading now.

if you are me,
sorry, it's cool

Dear Whoever Is Reading My Dumb Diary,

Are you sure you're supposed to be reading somebody else's diary? Have you done this before? If I did not give YOU permission, YOU had better stop right now.

If you are my parents, then, YES, I know that I am not allowed to call people idiots and fools and goons and half-wits and gerds and all that, but this is a diary, and I didn't actually "call" them anything. I *wrote* it. And if you punish me for it then I will know that you read my diary, which I am *not* giving you permission to do.

Now, by the power vested in me, I do promise that everything in this diary is true, or at least as true as I think it needs to be.

Signed,

Jamie Kelly

PS: If this is you, Angeline, reading this, then you are officially busted. I happen to have this entire room under hidden video surveillance. And, in just a moment, little doors will slide open and flesh-eating rats will stream into the room. And, like tiny venomous cowboys, scorpions will be riding the rats. So it's curtains for you, Angeline! Mwah-hah-hah-hah!

SNIP

I love Animals

PPPS: If this is you, Isabella, don't you ever get tired of reading my diary? I mean, I've caught you doing it, like, nine or ten times, so just STOP IT. Seriously. <u>Maybe</u> you should see somebody about this.

Dear Jamie-
I am <u>so</u> sure. I do <u>NOT</u> read your diary. So get over yourself.

—Isabella

PS- I totally agree with the stuff you said about your mom.

Sunday 01

Dear Dumb Diary,

Mom and I got into a "discussion" about fashion after dinner tonight. Of course, she really has no idea what the trends are at my school. I told her that I think she can't possibly know how important trends can be, and she said that clothes were just as important when she was in middle school. Then I said that I understood how she probably always tried her best to make a good impression on Fred and Wilma and Barney and the whole gang down at the tar pit, but times had changed.

a typical mother-daughter discussion

And that's just part of the reason I'm here in my room way ahead of schedule for the evening. Here's the exchange that followed my Mom-Is-Old-As-Cavemen joke:

"Just how do you think that makes me feel?" Mom asked.

"Stupid?" I guessed.

Turns out that Mom had a different answer in mind, and I'll have a little time to figure out what it was since I'm here in my bedroom about five hours earlier than usual.

I also think that Dad sitting there trying *not* to laugh might have made things worse.

You can always tell when Dad is trying not to laugh

Sometimes diaries can be so much easier to talk to than moms. I can't picture Mom letting me write on her face, and I imagine sliding a bookmark in somewhere would result in a major wrestling match.

Monday 02

Dear Dumb Diary,

Angeline is back to her old tricks, Dumb Diary.

Yeah, sure, for a long time, everything was fine between us. (Nearly four whole days — except two of those were over the weekend, during which I did not see her.) But then today, in science class, while I was talking to Hudson Rivers (eighth cutest guy in my grade), she performed an act of **UTTER BEAUTY** and distracted him.

Actually, I hadn't started to talk to him yet, but I was going to, and she should have known that when she whipped out her **GORGEOUSNESS** and waved it all over the place.

Isn't it time we stopped the beautiful people?

It's true. I may not be fully qualified to talk to Hudson Rivers. Maybe he *is* just slightly too cute for me. (I'm right on the edge of adorable.) But if I'm really, really lucky and keep my fingers crossed, he could become mildly disfigured. Then we'd be on the same level, and I want to make sure I'm ready should that blessed maiming occur.

And, besides, Angeline is in that Mega-Popular category where she can probably go and work her wicked charms against boys like Chip, who is the number-one cutest boy in the school.

So why does she always have to perform acts of **Beauty** around Hudson?

(Chip, like Madonna and Cher and Moses, only goes by his first name. I'm not sure anybody knows what his last name is.)

other one-Namers

PINK

TARZAN

BEEPY

THE SCIENCE OF BOY-OLOGY
Local Specimens

CHIP
CUTENESS RANKING: **1**

NON-MEAN AND HANDSOME ENOUGH TO BE IN A SHAVING CREAM COMMERCIAL

HUDSON RIVERS
CUTENESS RANKING: **8**

EASILY TRICKED INTO THINKING ANGELINE IS PRETTY. OTHERWISE EXCELLENT

ROSCO (CHIP'S DOG)
CUTENESS RANKING: **19**

STRICTLY SPEAKING NOT A BOY, BUT CUTER AND WAY MORE POPULAR THAN MOST TRUE BOYS

MIKE PINSETTI
CUTENESS RANKING: **ALMOST LAST**

MEAN AND MOUTHY. IF YOU MEET HIM TELL HIM ALL ABOUT SOAP.

THAT ONE KID
CUTENESS RANKING: **LAST**

DOES HE EVEN HAVE A NAME? WHO KNOWS. HE DOESN'T SEEM TO NEED ONE

It all started with a Scarecrow.

Puffin is seventy years old.

Sounds ancient, doesn't it? But Puffin has never been
so lively. We're always on the lookout for the next big
idea, which is how it began all those years ago.

Penguin Books was a big idea from the mind of
a man called Allen Lane, who in 1935 invented
the quality paperback and changed the world.
**And from great Penguins, great Puffins grew,
changing the face of children's books forever.**

The first four Puffin Picture Books were hatched in 1940 and the
first Puffin story book featured a man with broomstick arms called
Worzel Gummidge. In 1967 Kaye Webb, Puffin Editor, started the
Puffin Club, promising to **'make children into readers'**.
She kept that promise and over 200,000 children became
devoted Puffineers through their quarterly instalments of
Puffin Post, which is now back for a new generation.

Many years from now, we hope you'll look back and
remember Puffin with a smile. **No matter what your age
or what you're into, there's a Puffin for everyone.**
The possibilities are endless, but one thing is for sure:
whether it's a picture book or a paperback, a sticker book
or a hardback, **if it's got that little Puffin
on it – it's bound to be good.**